William Bee's Wonderful World of
TRUCKS

Hello. I am William Bee, and this is my
Wonderful World of Trucks.

Trucks are the most useful of vehicles, and possibly the most useful of trucks is my fuel tanker. It carries all the fuel I need for my cars, and diggers, and tractors, and yes, all my trucks!

It carries enough fuel to fill up 2500 motorbikes, or 650 cars, or 40 of my biggest trucks.

Without this truck, none of the others would go.

Apart from this one, that is – it's my coal-fired steam truck.
It's perfect for when you want to go somewhere slowly,
make lots of smoke and blow a whistle that goes 'Peep! Peep'!

It's also perfect if you want to be covered all over in
dirty, dusty soot.

And so... it's bath time!

And this truck drives into the bath with you.

It's amphibious, which means it can swim.

Here at William Bee's Garage we are always putting up new buildings, so we can have even more trucks!

BUILDING SUPPLIES

WILLIAM BEE
BUILDING SUPPLIES

WILLIAM BEE
BUILDING SUPPLIES

WB 40/41

ELEPHANT
HYDRAULIC
FLUID

This is the truck that
carries all the bricks, and
the wood, and the pipes.
It has its very own crane.

This truck is full of wet cement.
The back goes round and round while it
drives along, mixing the cement
so it is ready for pouring when it gets
to the building site.

All that building work is hungry work.
So here's a truck that can cook your dinner,
and your lunch, and your breakfast, and your tea.

NTEATER
EDGEHOG
ADGER
NGUIN
RAFFE
AUSAGE
EGG

8

6

TODAY'S
SPECIAL

OUBLE SLUG & CHEESE
BURGER WITH
CRISPY WORM FRIES

WILLIAM BEE'S
CAFE TRUCK

DOG
MENU

DOG FOOD

Sometimes I get called out to rescue a truck.

Somewhere in this big,
brown, rusty, piled-up
mess of mangled metal
is a truck that needs rescuing.

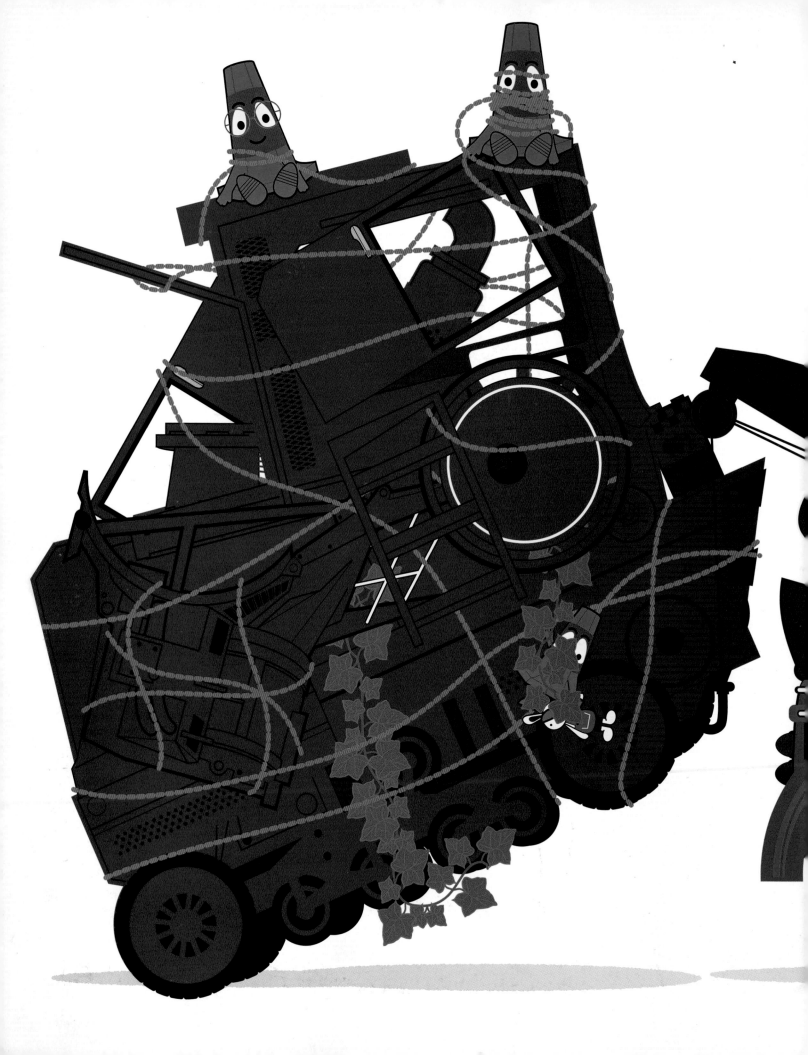

And this is my rescue truck.

After lots of cutting and banging
and twisting and drilling

and sanding and bolting and bashing and
riveting and welding and painting...

Hey presto!
We have a beautiful snow-blowing truck! It scoops up all the snow and blows it up high over the hedges.

Now all we need is some snow...

William Bee's Garage has lots and lots of racing cars, and sometimes – quite annoyingly – I have to take

three of them to the race track all at once.
Which would be difficult if it wasn't for my...

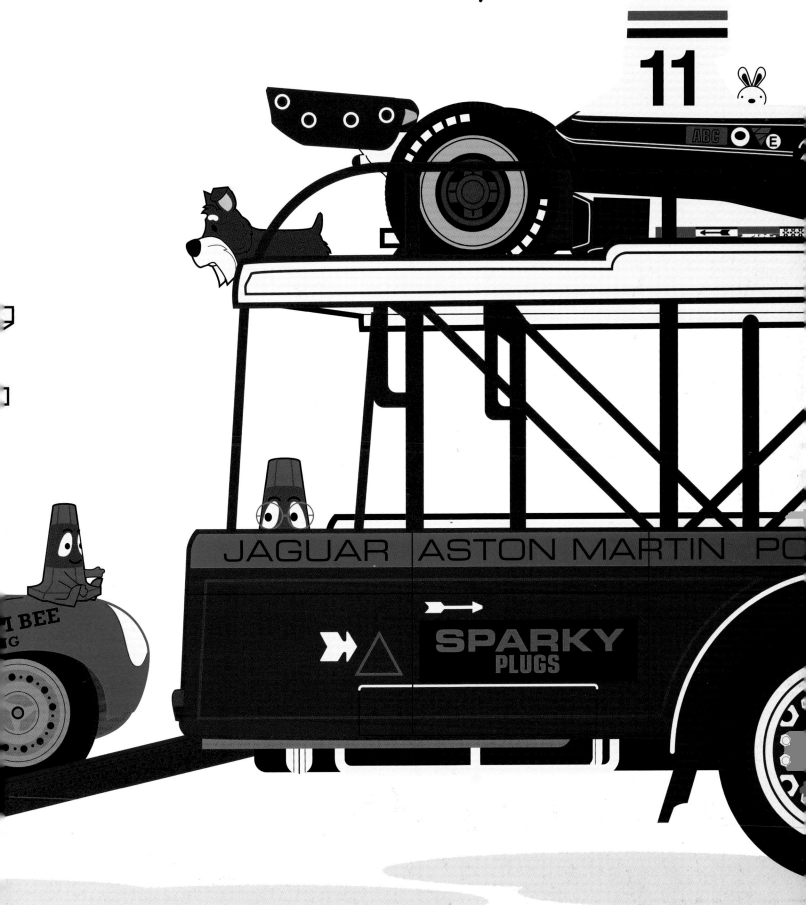

...racing car transporter, which can carry three racing cars all at once.

Inside there is plenty of room for spare wheels and tyres, for tool boxes, fuel cans and all those sticky numbers.

Of course, sometimes I might not want to race one of my racing cars; I might want to race one of my trucks – like this jet-powered truck.

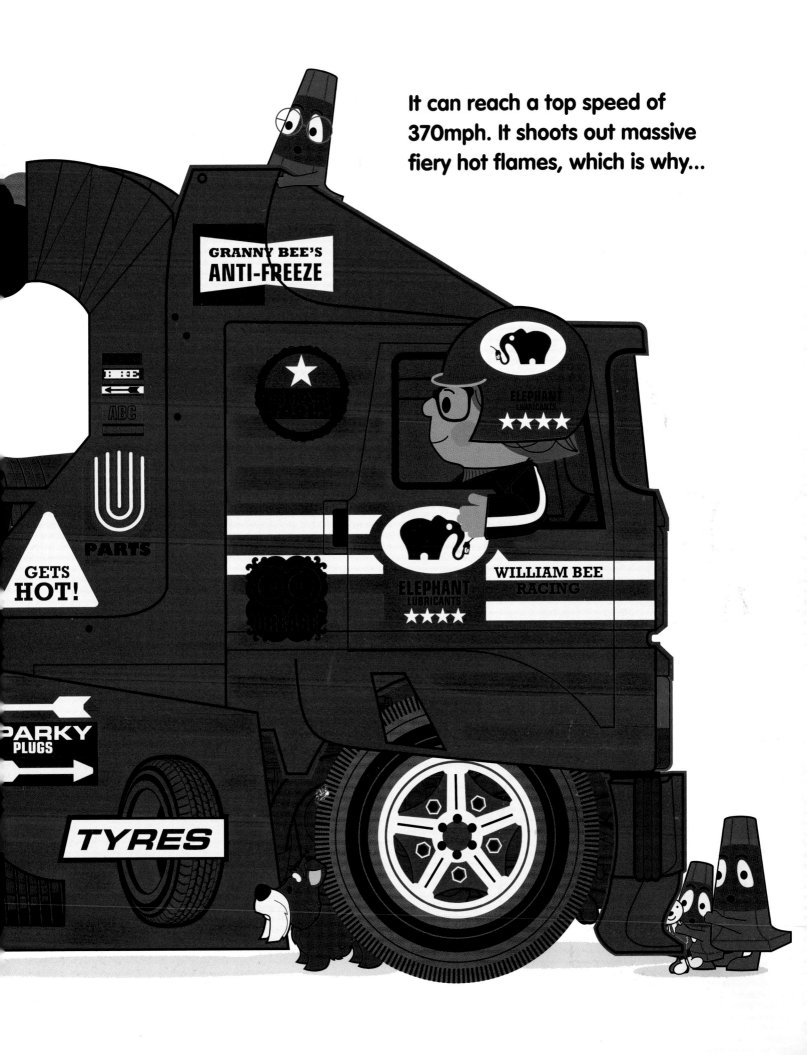

It can reach a top speed of 370mph. It shoots out massive fiery hot flames, which is why...

...it's always a good idea to have one of my many fire engines standing by, just in case.

WILLIAM BEE
FIRE
SERVICE

50

14 4545 6027

X 23P 1446

XL

Now I haven't got time to show you any more of my trucks, because we are off to the seaside in this one.

Which is a shame, because
I would have liked to show you
my tank-carrying truck,

and my fully-automated refuse truck,

and all my little trucks that can
whizz through little gaps,

not to mention my log-carrying truck,

and my giant tipper truck - so big
that this book would have to be
twice as high just to fit it in.

Maybe next time. Peep! Peep!

More truck facts from William Bee

So here it is – the biggest truck in the world!

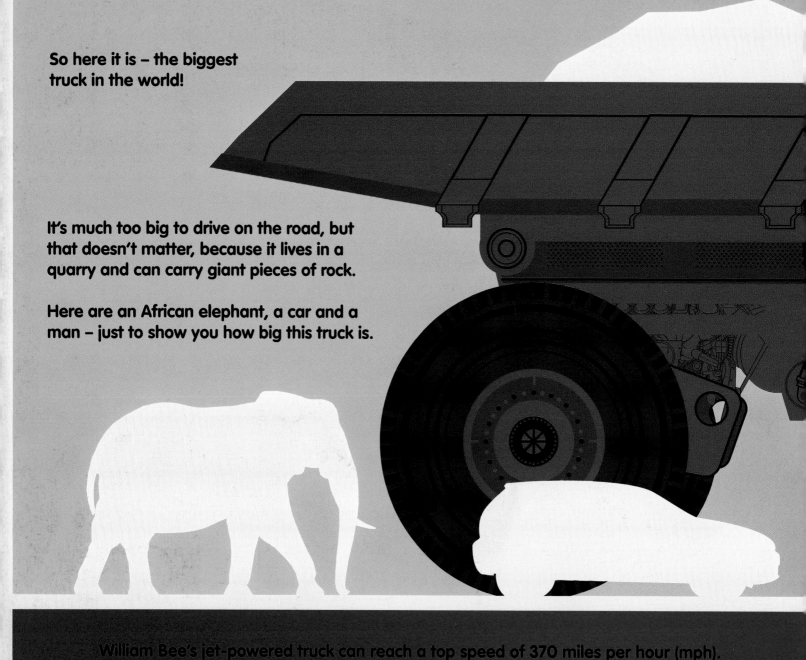

It's much too big to drive on the road, but that doesn't matter, because it lives in a quarry and can carry giant pieces of rock.

Here are an African elephant, a car and a man – just to show you how big this truck is.

William Bee's jet-powered truck can reach a top speed of 370 miles per hour (mph). An African cheetah has a top speed of 60mph – which is very fast if you haven't got an engine. A family car can reach a top speed of 130mph, but a really sporty car can manage 180mph. And a Formula One car? That can do 220mph.

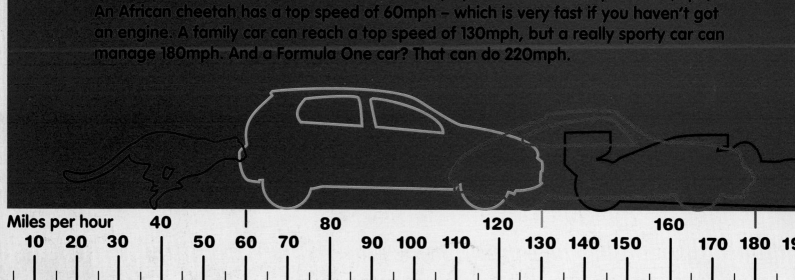

Miles per hour   40   80   120   160
10 20 30   50 60 70   90 100 110   130 140 150   170 180 19

WILLIAM BEE QUARRYING

The quarry truck driver has to climb up all these stairs to reach the cab.

ELEPHANT
LUBRICANTS

GRANNY BEE'S
ANTI-FREEZE

GETS
HOT!

SPARKY
PLUGS

TYRES

WILLIAM BEE

Trucks sometimes have a separate front and back. The front of the truck can be driven on its own. Some trucks have their engines underneath the driver's cab. The whole cab tilts forward – like this – so that a mechanic can reach the engine.

William Bee's fuel tanker carries three types of fuel all at the same time. Unleaded petrol goes into the green hatch, super-unleaded petrol goes into the red one, and diesel goes into the blue hatch.

STANDARD

ELEPHANT

ELEPHANT

ELEPHANT

★★★★

At William Bee's Garage there is a hole in front of each pump and a fuel tank underneath each one.

Some truck drivers drive over 125,000 miles a year. That is five times around the world, or halfway to the moon!

Many drivers sleep in their trucks. They might have a bed, a fridge, a microwave and a television in there to keep them happy.

Diesel goes in here,

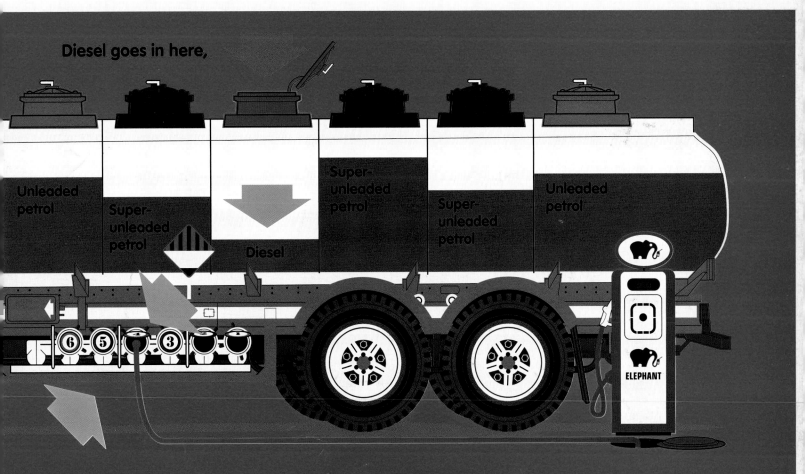

Unleaded petrol

Super-unleaded petrol

Super-unleaded petrol

Diesel

Unleaded petrol

Super-unleaded petrol

ELEPHANT

6 5 3

then comes out of here... and goes into a tank under the diesel pump.

William Bee recommends ELEPHANT PRODUCTS for all his trucks

If you enjoyed this book

William Bee's Wonderful World of TRUCKS

William Bee's Wonderful World of TRAINS and Boats and Planes

you might also like William Bee's Wonderful World of Trains and Boats and Planes,

William Bee's Wonderful World of TRACTORS and Farm Machines

or William Bee's Wonderful World of Tractors and Farm Machines